W9-CLO-988

COMUS

COMUS

ADAPTED BY
MARGARET HODGES
FROM
· A MASQUE AT LUDLOW CASTLE ·
BY
JOHN MILTON

ILLUSTRATED BY
TRINA SCHART HYMAN

HOLIDAY HOUSE · NEW YORK

To John Milton
M.H.

To Michou
T.S.H.

Text copyright © 1996 by Margaret Hodges
Illustrations copyright © 1996 by Trina Schart Hyman
All rights reserved
Printed in the United States of America
First Edition
Library of Congress Cataloging-in-Publication Data
Hodges, Margaret, 1911–
Comus / adapted by Margaret Hodges from A Masque at Ludlow Castle by
John Milton ; illustrated by Trina Schart Hyman. — 1st ed.
p.   cm. Summary: When Alice and her two younger brothers become lost in
the woods, the children separate, and Alice is captured by an evil
magician named Comus.
ISBN 0-8234-1146-X
[1. Brothers and sisters—Fiction.   2. Magic—Fiction.
3. Magicians—Fiction.]   I. Hyman, Trina Schart, ill.   II. Milton,
John, 1608–1674. Comus.   III. Title.
PZ7.H6644Co   1996   94-13618   CIP   AC
[E]—dc20

Once upon a time there were three children who lived with their father and mother in a castle at Ludlow, near the River Severn. Alice was the oldest. Then came John, then Thomas. In a wild woods not far from the river, the children often played hide-and-seek or roamed about, looking for flowers and berries.

But one day, as they went along and went along in the wild woods, they strayed too far from home. Night was falling, and the forest was closing in around them. Soon the path disappeared among dark bushes.

Alice sat down to rest under a tree. "I am too tired to go farther," she said to her brothers. "Perhaps you can find the path. I will wait here until you come back."

"We'll bring you some berries and some water to drink," said John, and off he went with Thomas. Soon their voices and footsteps died away.

All alone Alice waited and waited, but her brothers did not come back. Then in the distance she heard the shouts of a wild, savage crowd.

The noise seemed to be coming closer. Alice trembled, but she was too brave to cry. Suddenly there was silence. Looking into the darkness of the deep woods, Alice saw evil faces peering out, watching her, but she did not dare to move.

"Perhaps John and Thomas are not far off," she thought. "I'll sing to keep up my courage, and maybe my brothers will hear me."

But while Alice sang, someone else was listening and saying to himself, "Ah! My nightingale! I will catch you and keep you!" This was Comus, a wicked magician. The sounds Alice had heard were the voices of monsters, once men and women, whom Comus had turned into beasts. He had learned his spells from his mother, Circe, a witch, and his father, Bacchus, the god of wine.

Comus stepped toward Alice, throwing magic dust into the air so that her eyes were dazzled. To her he looked like a harmless villager, wearing a homespun cloak and carrying a staff. In the dark of night she did not see the two little horns among his thick curly locks or the cloven hooves below his shepherd's dress.

He greeted her courteously. "Lady, how came you to be in the wild woods all alone?"

"My brothers left me to rest here while they went to find water and some berries to refresh me," said Alice.

"Are they grown men or boys?" asked Comus.

"They are only lads," she told him.

"I saw two lads about nightfall, due west of here," said Comus. "They were a handsome pair and were picking berries. Let me help you find them."

"You must know the paths well to find the way on such a dark night," said Alice.

"I know all the paths," the stranger answered. "I will find your brothers, Lady, or if not, I can lead you to a humble but honest cottage where you will be safe."

"I trust your word," said Alice. "I know that simple folk are often more honest and courteous than great people at the king's court."

Soon after Comus had led Alice away, deeper into the woods, her two brothers returned to where they had left her.

"Where can she be?" Thomas said anxiously. "Is she wandering about in the dark and damp among sharp burrs and thistles? What if someone has stolen her away?"

"How will we ever find our way home? If only the moon or stars would shine!" John sighed. "If we could even see the flicker of one small candle among the trees!"

"If we could hear sheep bleating or a cock crowing, we would know we were near a shepherd's cottage," said Thomas. "But it is worse for Alice, all alone."

John answered, "Alice is not the sort to be afraid for no reason."

"True enough," said Thomas. "Only don't forget the old story about the dragon who guards the golden apple tree to keep it safe from robbers. Alice is beautiful, and beauty should be guarded."

"Still, let's hope rather than fear," said John. "I have heard that no evil spirit, no witch or ghost or goblin or wicked fairy, can harm a truly good person, as Alice is. Listen! I hear shouting far off."

"I hear it, too," said Thomas.

"Maybe it is someone lost, like us, or maybe a forester," John answered. "Unless it is a robber calling to other robbers."

"Heaven help my sister!" said Thomas. "There is the noise again, coming nearer. Let's draw our swords and stand on guard."

While the two brothers stood with swords drawn, someone came toward them. He looked like a shepherd, and Thomas thought that he had seen his face before. "What are you doing here, good shepherd?" he asked. "Have you come from Ludlow Castle, looking for a lost sheep, and found us instead?"

But this was not a shepherd. It was a Good Spirit who had come from the other end of the rainbow, sent from heaven to guard those in danger. He had taken off his rainbow robes and put on a shepherd's cloak.

"I did not come to find a lost sheep but to find you and your sister," he said. "Where is she?"

"We lost her, shepherd," said John. "It was not our fault."

"Then I'm even more fearful than before I met you," said the Spirit. "In the very center of these wild woods lives a powerful magician. Comus is his name. He is as skillful in witchcraft as his mother Circe, and, like his father Bacchus, he offers every thirsty wanderer a drink that changes a man or a woman into a monster with the face of a beast. When I tend my flocks on the hills at night, I can hear Comus's rabble, howling like wolves or tigers. Tonight I heard them again. Then suddenly they were silent and I heard someone singing as sweetly as a nightingale. I knew it was the voice of the Lady, your dear sister. Down the hill I ran until I found the place where that deceitful wizard must have met the innocent Lady. Of course she thought he was some good villager who would lead her to her brothers. I came swift as the sparkle of a star, but not swift enough."

"She's in danger!" cried Thomas. "John, you said no harm could come to her!"

"And I still say so!" John answered. "But let's go to her. I'll draw my sword against that cursed magician, even if he has all the grisly legions of hell around him!"

"I love your courage," said the Spirit. "But one wave of Comus's magic staff could take all your courage away. I must go with you."

"How can you help us?" asked John.

"I am carrying a little root called Haemony," said the Good Spirit. "It grows in our country fields, but though it is not beautiful and is dark and prickly, it has wonderful powers to protect anyone against enchantments. I will use it to open the door of Comus's hidden palace, and I will give each of you a piece of Haemony to carry with you."

"If you will open the door, we are not afraid to attack Comus by ourselves," said John.

"Then you must rush boldly in and break his crystal glass," the Spirit told him. "Attack Comus with your swords and seize his staff, for all his power is in the staff. You will not strike in vain, and once you have defeated Comus, his monsters will disappear like smoke. I will be nearby if you need me. You will see me again."

The Good Spirit showed the brothers a path through the woods to a round green hill. He touched it with the root of Haemony and a door opened into a dark passage. The Good Spirit disappeared, but John and Thomas went forward boldly. The door closed behind them.

There were neither windows nor candles in the passage, but in a strange kind of twilight the brothers could see that the walls and roof were thickly set with jewels. The air was warm. At the end of the passage the brothers stopped, half hidden in the shadows. Before them was a fantastic sight—a spacious hall, its roof supported by pillars of gold and silver wreathed with diamonds and emeralds, rubies and pearls. In the middle of the roof, hung from a golden chain, was a great lamp made of one enormous pearl in which a red jewel spun round and round, lighting the hall like a setting sun. Comus's monsters were crowded around tables of rich and delicious food. They were dressed in fine clothes with jeweled belts and sparkling embroideries, but above all the splendor, the faces of beasts—apes, and wolves, and hogs, and some beasts never known on land or sea—chattered and howled and grunted.

Then the two brothers saw Alice. In the midst of this fearful place, she sat on a high, carved chair, and Comus stood before her, holding out his crystal glass. He was no longer disguised as a kindly shepherd, but showed himself as he really was, a crafty demon.

"See, Lady, you cannot move from my enchanted chair," he said. "I have caught you, my nightingale, and if I wave my staff, you will never move again. But if you drink from my glass, all my riches are yours. You will be queen in this palace, and happier than you have ever been."

"You lie," said Alice bravely. "Was this the safe cottage you told me of? Who are these monsters? You want to trap me as you have trapped them. I will not touch your food and drink. If I do, you will keep me here forever. Heaven help me!"

Again Comus held out his glass, smiling.

"Come," he said, "no more of this nonsense. Take one sip!"

At this, the brothers rushed in with swords drawn. They seized Comus's glass and hurled it to the floor, breaking it into a thousand pieces.

"We know who you are!" they cried. "Come and face us, foul fiend!"

But Comus, waving his staff, fled with his monsters into a dark tunnel and was gone.

Just then the Good Spirit appeared. "The false enchanter was too quick for you," he said to the brothers. "He has escaped with his staff and taken his wicked power with it. And there sits the Lady, bound by a spell that even Haemony cannot break. But wait! There may be another way. Not far from here, in the river Severn, lives a gentle nymph who is as powerful as Comus. Her name is Sabrina, goddess of the stream. Perhaps she can unlock the charm and free the Lady. I'll call her."

And by good magic, as the Spirit called, a sweet voice answered, clear as rippling water, "I am here." It was Sabrina herself, who had come in time of need, kind and smiling, surrounded by bright water nymphs, into the dark magic of Comus's palace. Sabrina sprinkled drops of pure water on Alice's eyes and ears, on her nostrils, lips, and fingertips. Then she laid her cool, moist hands on the enchanted chair, and Alice rose.

Free and unharmed, she ran to kiss her brothers, and to thank Sabrina.

"Come, Lady," said the Good Spirit, "we must fly from this cursed place. I will lead you safely home to your father's castle, where all are waiting for you anxiously."

Back they went together through the dark passage, into the wild woods, by easy paths to Ludlow Castle, into the arms of their father and mother. The whole countryside rejoiced that the children had been found.

The Good Spirit, his task done, waved farewell, and the children saw him in his rainbow robes, flying up to his own home in the blue field of the sky.

As for Alice and John and Thomas, in later years they sometimes ventured into the wild woods, but they never again saw Comus.

Author's Note

The oldest of all the old English fairy tales may be the one called "Childe Roland." The poet John Milton liked the story so much that he retold it as a play, which he called "a masque" because it was full of disguises.

Three children, Alice and John and Thomas Egerton, acted in the play, which was performed for the first time in their father's castle at Ludlow on Michaelmas Night, 1634. This was a festival day in England.

Alice played the part of The Lady. John and Thomas were The Two Brothers. Their music teacher, Henry Lawes, was The Good Spirit. We do not know who acted the part of Sabrina, the nymph of the river Severn that flows near Ludlow Castle. A professional actor may have played the part of Comus, the wicked wizard.

The towers of Ludlow Castle still stand, *Comus* is still performed there to this very day, and the story lives on forever.

M.H.